Bello the Cello

WRITTEN BY

Dennis Mathew

ILLUSTRATED BY

Samantha Kickingbird & Justin Stier

atmosphere press

ATMOSPHEREPRESS.COM

This book is dedicated to my wife Sini Mathew,
my constant voice of encouragement.

Bello the Cello was thrilled about his first day of school.

His teacher, Ms. Melody, was a treble clef,
full of joy and magic.
Walking into her room was like looking into other worlds.
Giant color patterns on the walls moved to music.

Bello and his friends walked into their new classroom with wonder-soaked gasps.

"To make new friends," Ms. Melody said,
"I want us to go around the room,
say our names and sing our songs!"

Bello wrinkled his brows. He twisted his lips.
He didn't know what kind of song he would sing.

"Hi! I'm Timmy the tambourine!"
said an energetic, thin fella.

He had shiny, flat, coin-like things
hanging off his body.

In a high pitched voice
he said, "When I move my body
and hit my drummytum, see what happens!"

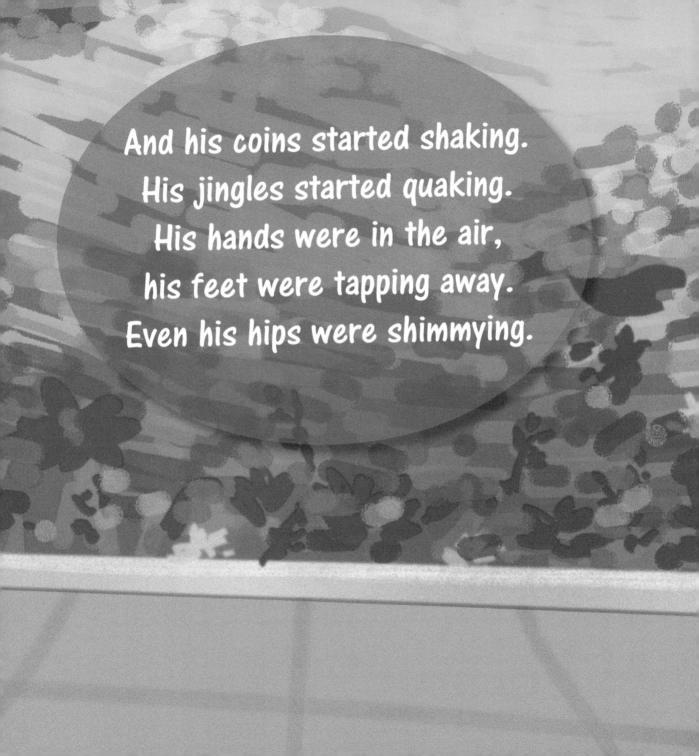

And his coins started shaking.
His jingles started quaking.
His hands were in the air,
his feet were tapping away.
Even his hips were shimmying.

"Hello! – I'm Finnegan 'the Flute' Flooterson," said a tiny little flute with beaming pride.

"I come from a prestigious family of..."

"Fluuuutes," the class filled in.

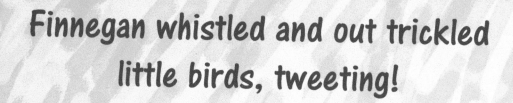

Finnegan whistled and out trickled
little birds, tweeting!

Ms. Melody started snapping.

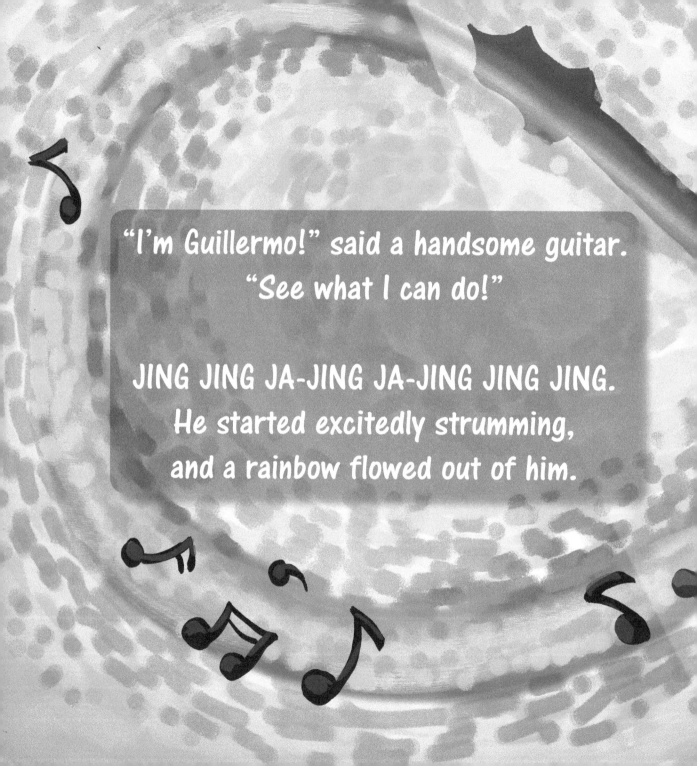

"I'm Guillermo!" said a handsome guitar.
"See what I can do!"

JING JING JA-JING JA-JING JING JING.
He started excitedly strumming,
and a rainbow flowed out of him.

Sierra the Saxophone illuminated the floor with circles of blue.

Pauley the Piano's keys lit up into colors when he played.

Deeya the Drum's rhythms even made a bright
and glorious sun appear smiling over them.

"Are you going to be joining your friends, Bello?

We'd love to hear you sing."

"Maybe a little later?" Bello said
with hesitation in his voice.

"But does my song have magic?" he wondered.

"It doesn't even sound like theirs," he thought.

Later, while everyone was at recess,
Bello was helping get the room ready for naptime.

"You're very considerate, Bello," a voice said gentl
Bello startled. Quietly, he turned around.

And there he was. So big. So bright.
The moon.

"Mr. Moon," Bello said, "my friends sing
and it makes everyone dance.
I don't know how to make my song fit in,
because my song doesn't sound like theirs."

Beaming down, Mr. Moon said,
"It's not about what you can't do
but rather about what you can do.

Bello, what can your song do?"

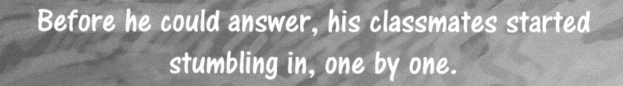

Before he could answer, his classmates started
stumbling in, one by one.

"I'm ready for my nap," said Guillermo the Guitar.
"My legs are tired from all that running,"
said Deeya the Drum.

Bello's friends started laying down to nap.
But they couldn't quite fall asleep.

Then, suddenly, like a light bulb turning on, like
a matchstick-spark, like a bubble-pop, Bello had an idea.

"What can your song do?" echoed in Bello's mind.

A smooth and deep, soothing song slowly filled the room.
It was very calming. It was Bello.

His friends started closing their eyes one by one.
Peace and quiet flooded Ms. Melody's room.

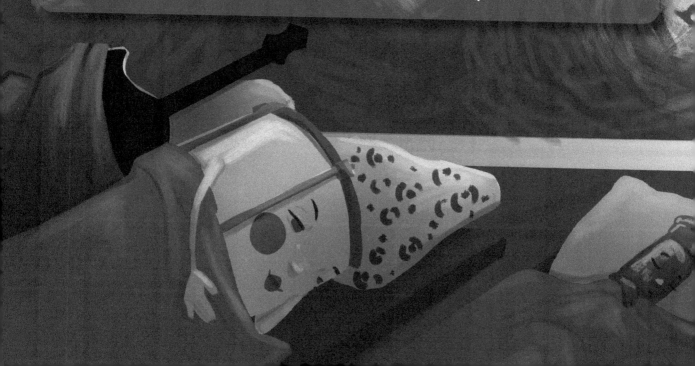

After everyone was asleep
Bello quietly laid down too

He knew he had found his song.

Dennis Mathew, a speech pathologist who has been working in elementary school for over 10 years, realizes his life-long dream of becoming a children's book author with Bello the Cello. He enjoys writing to encourage the everyday young underdog who strives to realize his or her God-given potential. Dennis aims to inspire wonder in the minds of his readers, to look at the world through the innocent and limitless mind of a child.

Breadcrumbs Ink, is a pair of illustrators working together to bring stories to life. Located in Oklahoma City, Justin Stier and Samantha Kickingbird worked together on many books before establishing their collective in 2014. If they were each a musical instrument, Samantha would be a Violin and Justin would be a Xylophone.

Atmosphere Press is an independent full-service publisher for books in genres ranging from non-fiction to fiction to poetry, with a special emphasis on being professional, honest, and kind. Atmosphere Press' latest releases are available at Amazon.com and via order from your local bookstore, and you can learn more about Atmosphere at atmospherepress.com.

CPSIA information can be obtained
at www.ICGtesting.com
Printed in the USA
BVHW051943181220
595721BV00002B/12